A FROG and DOG book

# Goat in a Boat

by Janee Trasler

ACORN™
SCHOLASTIC INC.

# For Jason, my favorite bunny guy.

Library of Congress Cataloging-in-Publication Data

Names: Trasler, Janee, author, illustrator. Title: Goat in a boat / Janee Trasler.
Description: First edition. | New York : Acorn/Scholastic Inc., 2020. |
Series: A Frog and Dog book ; [2] | Audience: Ages 4–6. | Audience: Grades K–1. | Summary: When Goat appears wearing a raincoat and invites all the animals to go for a boat ride on a sunny day, Dog declines but as heavy rain falls, Dog needs a boat, too. Identifiers: LCCN 2019048955 | ISBN 9781338540420 (paperback) | ISBN   9781338540451 (library binding) Subjects: CYAC: Rain and rainfall–Fiction. | Boats and boating–Fiction. | Floods–Fiction. | Frogs–Fiction. | Dogs–Fiction. | Friendship–Fiction.
Classification: LCC PZ7.T6872 Go 2020 | DDC [E]–dc23
LC record available at https://lccn.loc.gov/2019048955ISBN

10 9 8 7 6 5 4 3 2 1                                                 20 21 22 23 24
Printed in China                                                     62
First edition, May 2020

Edited by Rachel Matson
Book design by Sunny Lee

Goat

Frog

Frog

Frog

1

Here comes Goat.

5

6

7

8

Boat

Here comes Goat.

In a boat.

# Who wants a ride?

# Rain

Here comes the rain.

# Dog needs a boat.

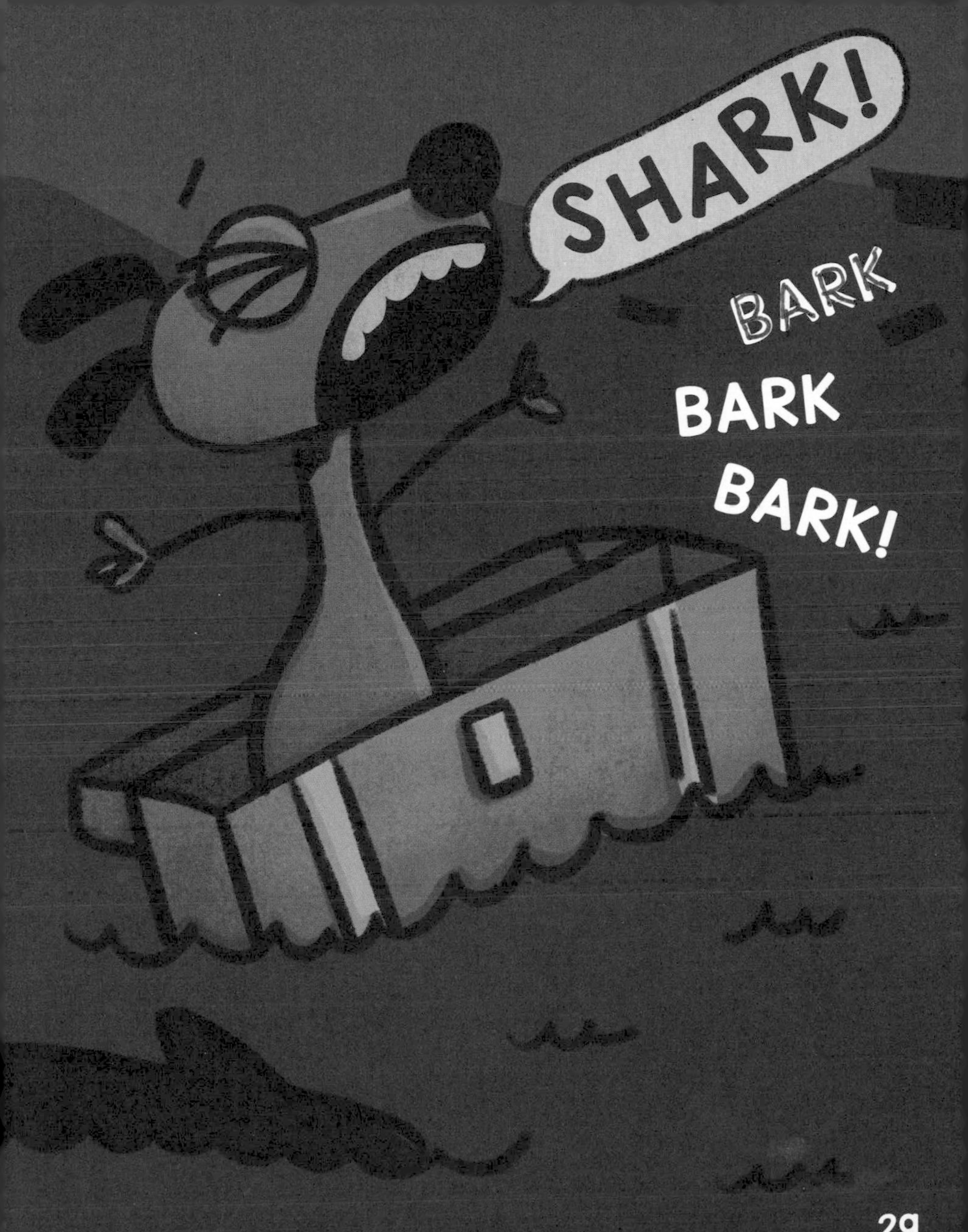
SHARK!
BARK
BARK
BARK!

It is not a shark.

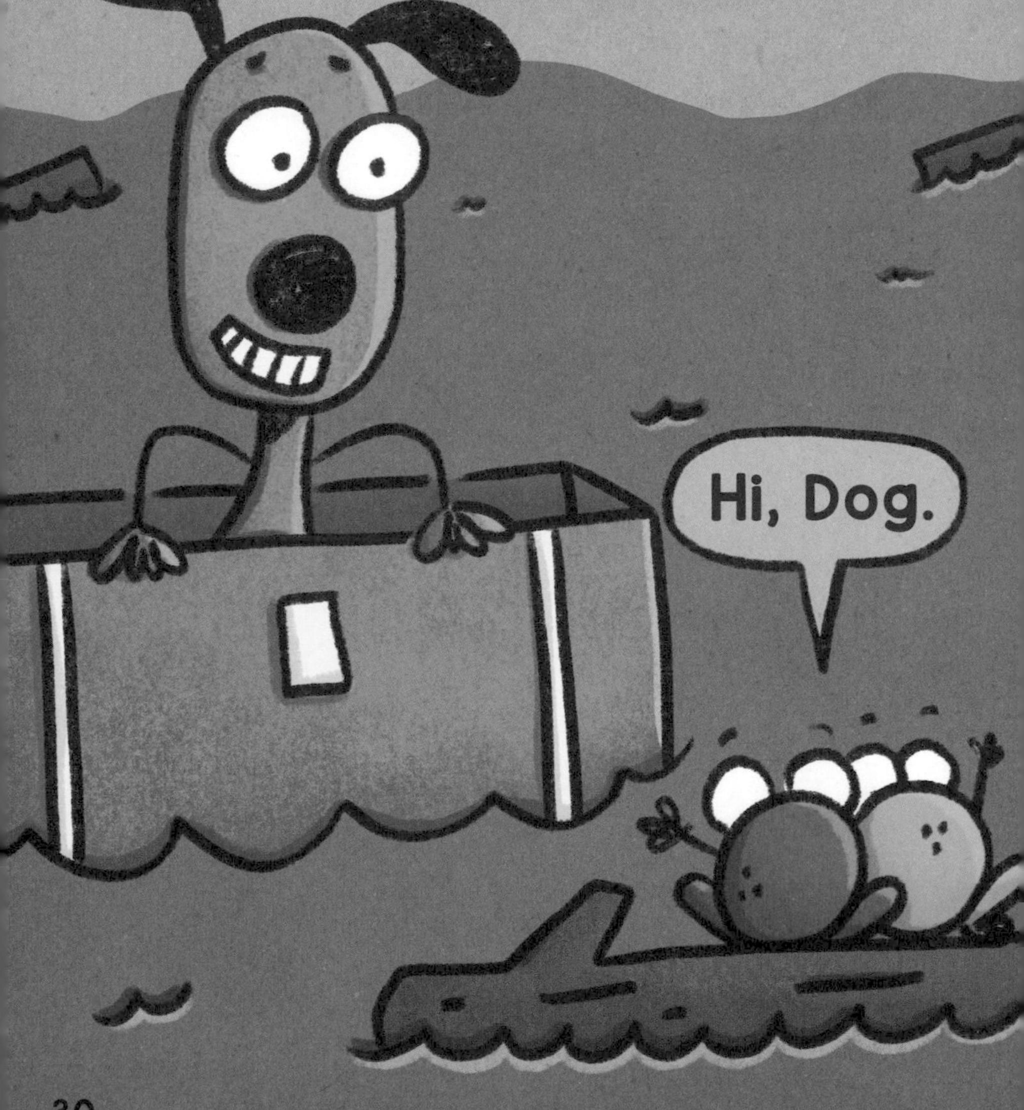

# Safe

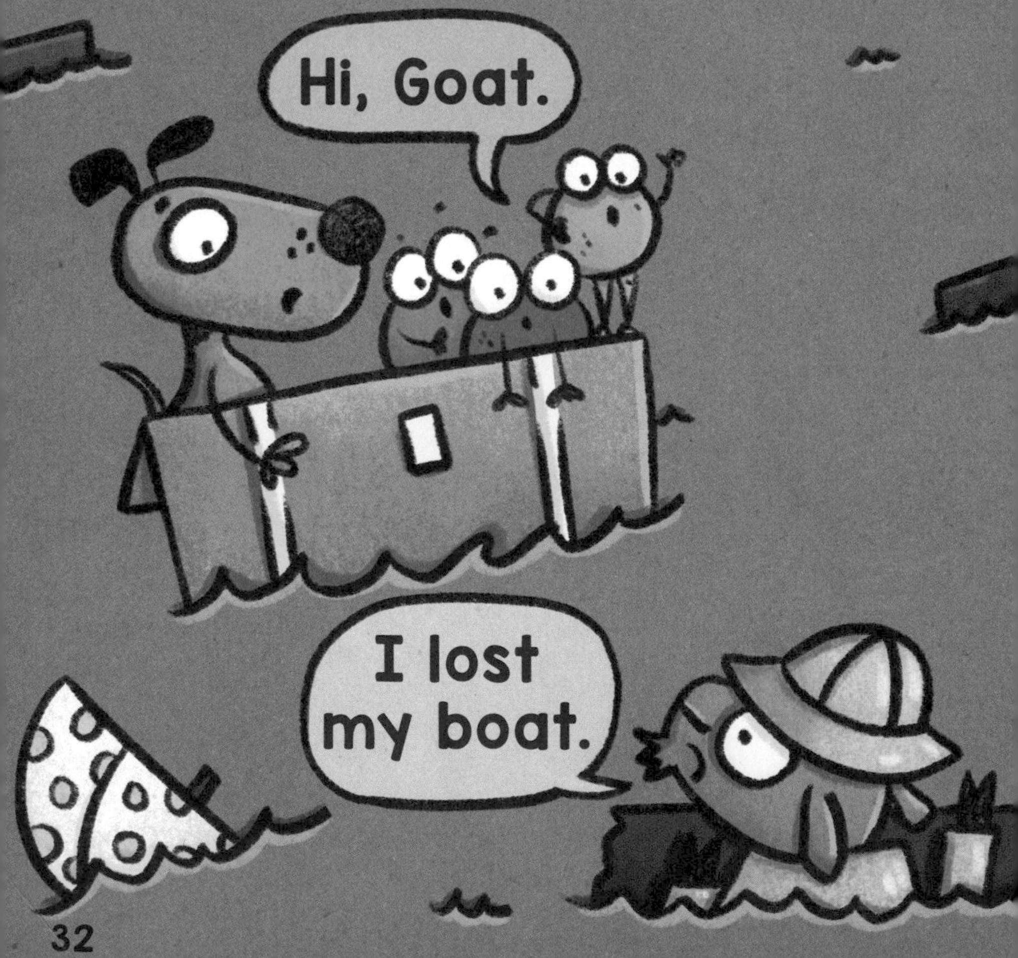

# Go Dog, go!

# Dog saves the day.

41